Welcome to ALADDIN QUIX!

If you are looking for fast, fun-to-read stories with colorful characters, lots of kid-friendly humor, easy-to-follow action, entertaining story lines, and lively illustrations, then **ALADDIN QUIX** is for you!

But wait, there's more!

If you're also looking for stories with tables of contents; word lists; about-the-book questions; 64, 80, or 96 pages; short chapters; short paragraphs; and large fonts, then **ALADDIN QUIX** is *definitely* for you!

ALADDIN QUIX: The next step between ready to reads and longer, more challenging chapter books, for readers five to eight years old.

Read all the ALADDIN QUIX books!

By Stephanie Calmenson

Our Principal Is a Frog!
Our Principal Is a Wolf!
Our Principal's in His Underwear!
Our Principal Breaks a Spell!

Royal Sweets
By Helen Perelman

Book 1: *A Royal Rescue*
Book 2: *Sugar Secrets*
Book 3: *Stolen Jewels*

A Miss Mallard Mystery
By Robert Quackenbush

Dig to Disaster
Texas Trail to Calamity
Express Train to Trouble
Stairway to Doom
Bicycle to Treachery
Gondola to Danger
Surfboard to Peril
Taxi to Intrigue

Little Goddess Girls
By Joan Holub and Suzanne Williams

Book 1: *Athena & the Magic Land*

Little
GODDESS
Girls
Persephone & the Giant Flowers

JOAN HOLUB &
SUZANNE WILLIAMS

QUIX

Ne... ...lhi

ALADDIN QUIX

Simon & Schuster Children's Publishing Division
1230 Avenue of the Americas, New York, New York 10020
First Aladdin QUIX paperback edition September 2019
Text copyright © 2019 by Joan Holub and Suzanne Williams
Illustrations copyright © 2019 by Yuyi Chen
Also available in an Aladdin QUIX hardcover edition.
All rights reserved, including the right of reproduction in whole or in part in any form.
ALADDIN and the related marks and colophon are trademarks of Simon & Schuster, Inc.
For information about special discounts for bulk purchases, please contact
Simon & Schuster Special Sales at 1-866-506-1949 or business@simonandschuster.com.
The Simon & Schuster Speakers Bureau can bring authors to your live event. For more
information or to book an event contact the Simon & Schuster Speakers Bureau
at 1-866-248-3049 or visit our website at www.simonspeakers.com.
Designed by Karin Paprocki
The illustrations for this book were rendered digitally.
The text of this book was set in Archer Medium.
Manufactured in the United States of America 0819 OFF
2 4 6 8 10 9 7 5 3 1
This book has been cataloged with the Library of Congress.
ISBN 978-1-5344-3109-6 (hc)
ISBN 978-1-5344-3108-9 (pbk)
ISBN 978-1-5344-3110-2 (eBook)

Cast of Characters

Persephone (purr•SEFF•oh•nee): A girl with flowers and leaves growing in her hair and on her dress

Athena (uh•THEE•nuh): A brown-haired girl who travels to magical Mount Olympus

Oliver (AH•liv•er): Athena's puppy

Zeus (ZOOSS): Most powerful of the Greek gods, who lives in Sparkle City and can grant wishes

Medusa (meh•DOO•suh): A

mean mortal girl with snakes for hair, whose stare can turn other mortals to stone

Hestia (HESS•tee•uh): A small, winged Greek goddess who helps Athena and her friends

Cerberus (SIR•ber•us): Hades's three-headed dog

Aphrodite (af•row•DIE•tee): A golden-haired, beautiful girl found in a large seashell

Hades (HAY•deez): Boygod of the Underworld in Greek mythology

Contents

1

Through the Crack

Whoosh! **Persephone**'s new friend, **Athena**, flew past her on golden winged sandals.

"Careful! You almost crashed into me!" Persephone shouted up to her. The leaves and flowers that grew from her dress fluttered wildly.

"Sorry!" Athena called back. "That's why I need to practice!"

The white wings at the heels of

her golden sandals whisked her back and forth. And then high in the air for a loop-the-loop.

Suddenly, the sandals took a big dive. Athena was zooming straight at Persephone now!

"Yikes!" Persephone leaped out of the way. The daisies that grew from the top of her head twirled.

"Slow down!" Athena told her sandals. For once, they obeyed. They floated her gently lower. Soon she was standing next to Persephone on the orange, blue, and pink Hello Brick Road.

"Wow," said Persephone. "Great landing! You're getting better!"

Athena smiled. "Thanks. There's no magic in the land I came from. Learning to fly is hard!"

"Woof! Woof!"

Oliver, Athena's little white dog, came bounding over. He'd been chasing butterflies. She scooped him up and gave him a big hug. Then he jumped down.

Athena and Persephone linked arms. They skipped down the road while Oliver trotted behind them. Up ahead they could see rainbow-colored sparkles. These were coming from Sparkle City, where they were heading. The city stood far away at the very top of magical **Mount Olympus**.

"Won't you miss flying if you leave Mount Olympus forever?" Persephone asked.

Athena nodded. "But I want to go home. **Zeus** *has* to help me." A storm had blown Athena to this magic land. Ever since, she had dreamed of getting back home.

"The super-duper powerful Zeus can do anything," Persephone promised. "He's king of the gods. We'll go see him in Sparkle City. I'm sure he'll give me the gift of good luck. And he'll help you get back home."

Persephone had bad luck-itis. Her bad luck was always rubbing off on others. So she really needed good luck. Besides, she loved growing things. With good luck she'd be able to help all plants grow strong and beautiful!

But the thought of Athena going home made her sad. Before they'd met, she'd never had a *girl* friend before. Only flower friends. Once her bad luck-itis was cured, she hoped the two of them would become *best* friends.

Persephone belonged here in Mount Olympus. She wished Athena would change her mind about going home. It would be great if she stayed here too!

"Hisss!" The girls jumped.

"Was that **Medusa**?" Persephone whispered. Medusa was a mean girl with wiggly green snakes for hair. She could turn you to stone with an eye zap! Had Persephone's bad luck-itis brought her?

"No! Look!" said Athena. She pointed up in a tree. There was a furry animal sitting on one of its branches.

"Woof! Woof!" barked Oliver.

"Hisss!"

"Phew! It's only a cat," said

Persephone. "I thought Medusa was back, trying to get her hands on your winged sandals."

Hestia, a tiny, fairylike goddess, had warned them not to let Medusa take Athena's sandals. Because the snake-haired girl might use their magic to make big trouble for Mount Olympus!

"Phew is right!" said Athena as they began walking again. "But as long as we stay here on the Hello Brick Road, that awful Medusa can't hurt us. An owl named Pink Tail told me that."

But Persephone was still worried. What if her bad luck-itis made the road lose its magic to keep them safe?

After a while the girls stopped to eat **pomegranates** from some trees at the side of the road. **Thump!** Out of nowhere, a **chariot** pulled by four black horses appeared. It came rolling across a field beyond the trees.

Athena scrunched her nose. "Hey! There's no one driving that."

Crack! To their surprise, the ground split open! Sparkles burst from the long crack that formed. The horses and chariot dove through it. They zoomed out of sight. The girls rushed over to the crack. They tried to see where the chariot and horses had gone.

"Woof!" Oliver ran to the crack too. Persephone scooped him up before he could fall into it. The girls stepped back as more sparkles burst up from below.

"Sparkles?" Persephone said in

excitement. "Maybe this crack is a shortcut to Sparkle City!"

"Maybe," said Athena. "Stay here. I'll go check."

"Wait! It might not be safe to follow that crazy chariot underground," Persephone said. She reached out and grabbed one of Athena's hands to stop her. She didn't want to lose her friend!

Too late! The sandals jerked and pulled them down through the crack! *Uh-oh!* Where were Athena's sandals taking them?

2

Cerberus

Athena, Persephone, and Oliver flew down, down, down underground. They spun around and around. It was a wild ride!

"Hold on tight!" Athena warned as her sandals zigzagged them left and then right.

It seemed to Persephone like the sandals had minds of their own! Who knew what else they could do. Or what other magic powers they held. No wonder Medusa wanted them so badly.

Thunk! Finally, the three of them landed near a big rock on the bank of a river. Both girls managed to land on their feet. Persephone handed Oliver to Athena.

"You okay, boy?" Athena asked him. She hugged him close. Oliver happily licked her face.

Not far ahead, Persephone could see a gate made of diamonds! Her heart sank. "Maybe the sparkles we saw through the crack were only these jewels," she said to Athena. "Not Sparkle City after all."

"Whoa!" a boy's voice shouted before Athena could reply.

Persephone and Athena peeked

out from behind the rock. The four black horses pulling the driverless chariot came to a stop before the gate. Suddenly a boy appeared, standing in the chariot. He had dark curly hair and was holding a shiny gold cap.

Persephone blinked. "Where did he come from?"

"I think maybe he was driving the chariot the whole time," said Athena. "But he was **invisible** before."

They watched the boy leap from

the chariot. He shoved his cap in a pocket. Then he clapped his hands together. The horses and chariot magically disappeared.

"That's a neat trick," whispered Athena.

"Yeah!" Persephone agreed.

The boy walked over to the gate.

"Hey! Think that gate might be a shortcut to Sparkle City?" Persephone asked. She wasn't ready to give up on the shortcut idea yet. The sooner they saw Zeus, the faster she would get her good luck!

"I hope so," said Athena. "Because we can't go back the way we came." She pointed up. The crack they had fallen through had sealed itself!

The girls started to leave their hiding place to follow the boy. But then a huge dog came racing toward the gate from the other side of it. They froze in place. Because not only was that dog big, it had three loud heads!

"*Growl. Bark! Roar!*"

Oliver perked his ears. "Grr."

"Shh," said Athena. "No

fighting. That big dog could eat you for breakfast."

"Yeah, like, in three bites," Persephone added. "Because it has three mouths!"

All six of the dog's eyes stared through the gate. It looked right at the rock they were hiding behind! Then the dog began to jump against the locked gate's bars. **"Growl. Bark! Roar!"**

Persephone giggled. She sometimes did that when she was super worried. "He can probably smell us."

"I hope we don't smell like dinner to him," Athena whispered.

The boy unlocked the gate with a big black key. "Chill, **Cerberus**," he said. "It's just me. And since I'm not wearing my cap of invisi-

bility, I know you can see me."

"So that's why we couldn't see him in that chariot!" Athena said.

"Another super neat trick," Persephone replied.

Creak. The boy pushed open the gate.

Persephone and Athena gulped. Would Cerberus escape? Were they about to become dog food?

No! The boy went through the gate and closed it behind him before Cerberus could get out. He gave each of his dog's three heads a pat. "Come on. Let's go home."

The boy headed off. The huge dog licked its chops and jumped at the gate one more time. Then it gave up and trotted after him.

Persephone breathed a sigh of relief. The girls waited till the coast was clear. Then they came out from behind the big rock.

Oliver leaped from Athena's arms. He ran up to the gate. "Wait for us," Athena told him.

"Woof!" Oliver replied. He wagged his tail and sat until the girls caught up to him.

There was a sign on the gate. Persephone read it aloud: "Wunder-world. Keep Out."

"Back home where I come from, 'wunder' is spelled with an o. Not a *u*," Athena remarked.

"It's spelled with an o here, too," Persephone replied. "I w-u-n-d-e-r what Wunderworld with a *u* is? Should we go find out?"

Athena frowned. "The sign says 'Keep Out.'"

"Yes, but it doesn't say, 'Athena

and Persephone, Keep Out,'" Persephone joked. She gave the gate a little push. It creaked open. "That boy forgot to lock the gate."

"Woof!" Before either girl could stop him, Oliver squeezed through the gate and ran off!

WUNDERWORLD

KEEP OUT!

3

Shell Shock

Persephone and Athena raced through the diamond gate after the little white dog.

"Stop, Oliver!" Athena called.

Oliver usually obeyed her. But this time he kept running.

Uh-oh, thought Persephone. Would Wunderworld bring them more bad luck?

They followed Oliver into a field of tall white star-shaped flowers called **asphodels**. Persephone had seen them in pictures, but never real ones. She would have liked to study them more closely. But there was no time!

"Oliver!" called Athena, huffing and puffing as they ran. "Where is he? I don't see him!"

"Probably because he blends in. A white dog in a field of white flowers," said Persephone.

The wings of Athena's sandals began to flap. "Grab on," she shouted. "My sandals will help us find him!"

Persephone took Athena's hand.

The sandals zoomed them up in the air.

"There he is!" Athena said, pointing. "Oliver!" she shouted.

They flew over him across the field, then past a river. Suddenly, yellow-orange flames shot from the river. It was on fire!

Beyond the river was a giant hole with a railing around it. And Oliver was headed right for it!

"Oliver, stop!" yelled Athena. Too late. He slipped under the railing and started to fall down the hole!

In the nick of time, the sandals swooped down. Persephone grabbed Oliver's red collar. "Gotcha!"

The girls flew back out and landed. Oliver leaped into Athena's arms, and she hugged him. He snuggled against her, looking tired from his run. "You shouldn't have raced off like that. You scared us!" she told him.

Persephone gave his head a scratch. "Yeah. You sure did." She stared into the hole. It was so deep, she couldn't see to the bottom.

There was a warning sign beside the hole. Athena read it:

"TARTARUS

"Only rotten people are
welcome here.
"If you are rotten—come in.
"If not—keep out for your
own safety!"

"Rotten? I guess that means Medusa would be welcome," joked Persephone.

Athena giggled. "But *we're* not rotten. And I don't want to meet anyone who is. Let's leave."

She set Oliver inside the book bag she carried. Its top flap was open. That way he could still peek out as they walked on.

Minutes later, they passed pretty purple-flowered bushes, and they heard chatting and laughing.

They saw a shining silver gate in the bushes. A sign on the gate read:

ELYSIUM

ONLY PERFECT PEOPLE

ARE WELCOME HERE.

IF YOU ARE NOT PERFECT—GO AWAY.

WE DON'T WANT YOU!

Persephone let out a huff. "*Nobody* is perfect! Maybe whoever is in there can tell us how to get to Sparkle City, though. Should we ask?"

"Worth a try," Athena agreed. They knocked and knocked on the gate. But no one answered.

"Never mind," said Persephone. "Whoever is inside is probably *perfectly* stuck-up!" Athena and

Persephone laughed.

The girls walked on. Minutes later, Athena stopped so fast that Persephone bumped into her. **Oomph!** They both stared at an amazing sight.

In front of them was a blue, heart-shaped sea no bigger than a swimming pool. And behind it stood a big golden palace.

They were just in time to see the chariot-boy and his big, scary dog disappear through the palace's front door. "Wow! That's their home?" said Athena.

Persephone cocked her head. "Do you hear singing?"

Athena listened, then nodded. "Where is it coming from?"

On sneaky feet, they tiptoed closer. Suddenly, a garden of colorful flowers shot from the ground and bloomed all around them.

"Wow! Those are giant flowers!" Persephone exclaimed.

"And they're singing!" Athena added.

The flowers' high, sweet voices

were in perfect **harmony**. They were singing a happy song:

It's a wonderful thing
To be able to sing
With a ring-a-ding-ding
And a la-di-la-ling!

Persephone looked around in wonder. She stood next to a clump of giant daisies that matched her hair. "Hey! Look at me. It's like when Oliver was in that field of white flowers. My hair and I blend right in. See?"

"Yes, you daisy-do," the giant daisies sang in her ear. They giggled.

Suddenly, a distant voice cried out.

"Help me! I'm trapped!"

"It's coming from that sea!" said Athena.

She and Persephone ran through the giant flowers. Out in the middle of the little sea, a small sea serpent was swimming around. It had shiny black scales.

Ick. Another snake, thought Persephone.

Athena called to it. "Hello! Did you just ask us for help?" It wasn't a silly question. As both girls knew, a lot of things in magical Mount Olympus land could talk. But the serpent was silent.

The distant cry came again. "Hey,

you guys! Help? Any day now!"

Persephone glanced in the direction of the voice. "Over there!" she said to Athena. She pointed to a gleaming white **scallop**-shaped shell. It was beautiful. The size of her hand, its two halves were closed tight.

Persephone and Athena stared at each other in surprise. Hestia had told them they would find a beautiful shell.

"You found me stuck in the muck," Persephone said to Athena.

"This shell is stuck too. In the middle of the sea."

"Right. We have to help it," said Athena. "Or whoever is inside it."

"Remember what else Hestia told us?" said Persephone. "If we tap on the shell three times, it'll open."

"Yeah, but Hestia also said we'd find troubles on our way to Sparkle City. What if this shell is full of trouble?"

"Hello?" the voice called out again. Sounding a little mad now,

it asked, "So are you going to help me or what?"

Persephone looked at Athena. "Should we?"

Athena shrugged, then nodded. Together they replied, "We will!"

4

Unshelled

"That shell is too far away for us to reach. And the sea looks pretty deep in the middle," Persephone said to Athena. She also didn't like the idea of wading into water with a sea serpent. Not even a small one!

"I have an idea," said Athena. She held up a stick Oliver had been playing with. "I think I can push the shell closer with this."

Athena carried the stick to the other side of the small sea. Then she gave the shell a hard push. It floated toward Persephone.

Athena ran back to join her. They watched the shell float closer. When it was only a couple of feet from shore, it stopped moving. But now it was close enough to reach.

"Do you want to be the one to tap on it?" Athena asked.

Persephone did. But she guessed Athena did too. "Let's both do it," she suggested.

"I don't care who does it. Just *hurry up!*" said the voice.

TAP!
TAP!
TAP!

"Cranky," Persephone whis-pered to Athena. They grinned at each other.

Athena held up the stick she'd used to push the shell. "Grab on," she said to Persephone. Together, they touched the shell with the tip end of the stick three times. **Tap! Tap! Tap!**

To their surprise the shell began to grow bigger and BIGGER. Soon it was the size of that Wunderworld chariot's wheel! *Whoosh!* It spun around. *Vrooom!* It zoomed toward the shore.

"Jump back!" yelled Persephone. They dropped the stick and leaped away before the shell could knock them over.

Once onshore the shell stopped spinning. Then it began to open up, like some giant book. Persephone and Athena held their breath, waiting to see what would be inside.

When the shell was fully open, Persephone exclaimed, "It's . . . a girl!"

The girl gracefully unfolded

herself from the shell. Out she stepped. She was the most beautiful girl Persephone had ever seen!

The shell girl looked about the same age as Persephone and Athena—eight years old. She had long golden hair. Her eyes were the color of a bright blue sky. She wore silver sandals and a blue silk dress that matched her eyes.

"Finally!" said the beautiful girl. "Am I glad to be out of that shell at last." She looked around her at the flowers, the sea, and the palace. "Where am I, anyway?"

"You are in Wunderworld," explained Persephone.

"Spelled with a *u*, not an *o*," added Athena.

The shell girl shrugged. "Never heard of it. Nice palace, though. Is it yours?" She stretched her arms over her head and bent from side to side.

"No, we're just visiting. Um, I'm Athena," said Athena.

"And I'm Persephone."

"Woof!" said Oliver.

"And that's my dog, Oliver," added Athena.

"Uh-huh," said the shell girl. She touched her toes.

When she said nothing more, Athena finally asked, "So what's *your* name?"

"If you must know, it's **Aphrodite**." She pulled one leg up to stretch it out. She really liked to exercise! Probably because she couldn't while in that shell.

Persephone pointed at it. "How did you get trapped in there?"

Aphrodite sighed. "Well, I was out walking yesterday when I met this girl. She had green snakes for hair, and—"

"Medusa!" Persephone and Aphrodite exclaimed together.

Aphrodite raised an eyebrow. "You know her?"

"She's bad news," said Athena.

"So what happened?" asked Persephone.

Aphrodite began to jog in place. "Well, I said something that made her mad. I do that a lot. People tell me I'm hard to like sometimes. Still, she started it."

"What did you say?" Persephone asked, curious.

Aphrodite's forehead wrinkled in thought. "The wind had tangled my hair a bit, and she asked if I was having a bad hair day. So I said, 'No, my hair is always per-fect. But I guess every day's a bad hair day for you, right?'"

The girls laughed.

Aphrodite's smile made her look more friendly. *Maybe Aphrodite will become my friend too*, thought Persephone. *Then I'll have two non-flower friends.*

"I thought it was funny too," Aphrodite said. "But Medusa didn't. She yelled that she would eye zap me to stone! Only for some reason her eye zap wasn't working. So she trapped me in a magic shell instead."

"How did you get here though?" asked Athena.

"No clue." That said, Aphrodite began to turn cartwheels.

"Maybe Medusa saw a crack in the ground like we did. Maybe she threw the shell into it," Persephone whispered to Athena.

"I bet you're right," Athena whispered back. "And the shell landed in this sea."

"*Growl. Bark! Roar!*"

The three girls jumped in alarm. *Uh-oh.* Cerberus was back! He came racing from the palace toward them.

Athena quickly grabbed up Oliver. As Cerberus got closer and closer, they could see his sharp, pointy teeth.

"We're all goners!" Persephone wailed. "Three girls equals one snack for each of that dog's mouths. And Oliver will be dessert!"

But then Aphrodite stepped up. "Stop that noise, you!"

Looking surprised, Cerberus

stopped mid-growl. Then they heard a sharp whistle. The boy ran out of the palace. "Sit!" he called to Cerberus. The dog sat.

The boy marched over to the girls. "What are you doing here?" he demanded.

"We saw your chariot go down through a crack in the ground," Athena told him. "We followed it. Then my little dog ran in through the front gate."

"We didn't mean to **trespass**," Persephone added. "But we were wondering. Is this a shortcut to Sparkle City?"

The boy looked confused.

"We're on our way there," Athena explained.

"If anybody cares, I arrived by shell," said Aphrodite, pointing.

"However you all came, you need to leave," the boy said gruffly. "You don't belong in Wunderworld."

He clapped his hands. Immediately his chariot and black horses appeared beside a clump of giant daisies. The same daisies that had spoken to Persephone earlier.

"Hop in," the boy said after leaping into the driver's seat. "I'll take you back up to the Hello Brick Road."

Athena climbed in first with

Oliver. Then Aphrodite. Cerberus tried to get in too. The boy shook his head. "No, boy. Go home!" The huge dog whined, but he jumped back down.

Before Persephone could climb aboard, the daisies whispered in her ear again. "Don't leave," they begged. "Stay here with us. Put down some roots."

"Sorry, I can't," she said kindly. But when she tried to take another step, she couldn't. The giant daisies had wound their stems around her legs! Their roots curled around her feet.

Suddenly, the black horses began to gallop. The chariot rose into the air. The others were leaving without her! They hadn't seen what was happening.

Her bad luck-itis had struck again!

5

Onward

All at once the flying chariot made a U-turn. It headed back Persephone's way. The horses set down near her, and the chariot rolled to a stop. Athena, Aphrodite, and Oliver jumped down from the chariot and ran toward her.

"We didn't mean to leave you," Athena called. "**Hades** didn't realize you weren't on board!"

"*Hades?* Who's that?" said Persephone. But the daisies had put their petals over her mouth, so her words sounded like "**mmmpf**."

The chariot-boy had understood her, however. "Me! *I'm* Hades!" he called out to her.

When the girls and Oliver reached Persephone, they got to

work. Oliver dug near her rooted feet. Athena and Aphrodite unwound stems from her legs.

"Let go of her, you silly daisies!" Aphrodite shouted. "Don't make me break your stems!"

Hearing this, the giant daisies finally let go of Persephone. They sang:

We're very sorry!
*Didn't mean to **offend**.*
We were just hoping
to make a new friend.

"You can't *make* someone be your friend," said Persephone. "And it's not fair to keep someone away from their other friends."

As the words left her mouth she began to wonder. She hoped Athena and Aphrodite would decide to be best friends with her. But if they didn't, she'd have to accept that, hard as it would be.

Quickly the three girls and Oliver ran to the chariot. After they got in, the horses galloped upward again.

"Open!" yelled Hades. At his command, a new, big crack opened overhead. They zoomed up and out through it. A moment later, the horses and chariot landed on the Hello Brick Road.

The girls hopped out with Oliver. "Thanks for the ride!" they told Hades.

He waved good-bye. Then he drove his horses and chariot back down through the crack. It closed behind them.

Persephone gazed at the top

of Mount Olympus and frowned. "Sparkle City still looks far away."

"Yes, but it's nearer than when we followed Hades into Wunderworld," said Athena. "So it did turn out to be a shortcut after all."

"Still, we'd better get going if we're ever going to make it," said Persephone. She set off, moving fast. She needed Zeus's gift of good luck before her bad luck-itis could strike again. Next time it might bring something worse!

"Why are you both going to

Sparkle City?" Aphrodite asked as they walked along.

Athena answered first. "I don't belong here," she said. "I landed in magical Mount Olympus during a weird storm. My real home is far away. I'm going to ask Zeus to help me get back there. I heard he can help."

Aphrodite nodded. "Everyone says he's super-duper powerful."

"I'm going to ask him to give me good luck," said Persephone.

"Good idea," said Aphrodite.

"After seeing what those daisies did, I guess you could use some."

Persephone laughed. She and Athena looked at each other and smiled. *Were they both thinking the same thing?* Persephone wondered. *Like friends often did?*

"Want to come with us?" Athena asked Aphrodite. It was what Persephone had been thinking of asking too!

Aphrodite's blue eyes lit up. "Really? But are you sure? I can be hard to like. Sometimes I say things that hurt people's feelings. Not on purpose. It's just that I speak before I think."

"That's okay. Nobody's perfect," said Persephone. Besides, Aphrodite had helped rescue her. Which had been kind. And kindness was a likable quality.

Athena snapped her fingers. "I have an idea," she said to Aphrodite. "If you come with us, you could ask Zeus to give you the gift of, um, *likability*."

Aphrodite grinned. "I *like* it!"

The three girls linked arms and began to skip along the road. However, they'd only gone a few skips, when they heard a terrible cackle. **"Eee-heh-heh!"**

Uh-oh, thought Persephone. Her bad luck-itis was back already. Perched on a white fence at the side of the road was the snaky-haired Medusa!

6

Green Smoke

Medusa's zappy eyes did a double take when she noticed Aphrodite. "Well, well, well," she said. "Look who escaped her jail shell!"

"Look who's still having a bad hair day!" Aphrodite shot back.

Persephone giggled. But it was a worried giggle. Were they ever going to get to Sparkle City?

"**Grrr**," growled Oliver.

Medusa switched her gaze to Athena. "Give me those sandals and you'll never have to see me again."

"Ooh. Interesting offer," Aphrodite said to Athena. "But, no."

"Good," said a new voice.

"Hestia!"

Persephone and Athena exclaimed. The tiny, glowing, fairy-like goddess had popped out of nowhere. Now she hovered in the air between the four girls, wings flapping gently.

"Off with you, troublemaker!" she told Medusa. "Your magic is no use here. As long as these girls stick to the Hello Brick Road they are protected from harm."

Medusa let out another cackle. **"Eee-heh-heh!"** Ignoring the tiny goddess, she glared at the girls. "You won't be able to stay

on the road forever," she warned.
"And when you leave it, you'll be
at my **mercy**!" She cackled again.
"Too bad for you I don't *do* mercy!"
The snakes flicked their tongues

and hissed. Then Medusa disappeared in a puff of green smoke. *Poof!*

"Bye! We'll miss you. Not!" Aphrodite called after her cheerfully.

That girl was funny, thought Persephone. And, like kindness, funny was a likable quality.

Hestia's glow began to blink.

"Uh-oh," said Athena. "That means she is about to disappear."

"She tries to help us. But she can never stay for more than a few minutes at a time before she blinks away," Persephone added.

"Listen up," Hestia said quickly. "If all goes well you'll reach Sparkle City soon. But there's danger ahead. Watch out for—" She broke off as her glow blinked faster.

They all leaned closer. "For what?" asked Persephone.

But it was too late. *Pop!* The tiny goddess was gone.

"She isn't actually very helpful, is she," said Aphrodite.

Persephone shrugged. "You still

want to go with us? Even though it might be dangerous?"

"It's okay if you've changed your mind," Athena said kindly.

"Ha! Danger won't scare *me* off! Not a hissy mean girl either," Aphrodite declared.

Persephone giggled. Only it was a happy giggle this time. Because in her heart she knew for sure she had made two new *girl* friends. Maybe even *best* friends. How cool was that?

As the three girls linked arms

and began to skip, Persephone stared ahead at Mount Olympus. The rainbow-sparkles of Sparkle City looked closer than ever. They might find danger as they went on their way. But with the help of her new friends, she'd be up to the **challenge**!

Word List

asphodels (AS•fuh•dels): Flowers that grow in the Underworld

challenge (CHAL•enj): A test of someone's ability

chariot (CHAIR•ee•ut): A two-wheeled horse-drawn cart

harmony (HAR•mo•nee): Pleasing blend of music notes

invisible (in•VIZ•ih•bel): Not able to be seen

mercy (MER•see): Under someone else's control

Mount Olympus (MOWNT oh•LIHM•pus): Tallest mountain in Greece

offend (uf•END): Make someone mad or unhappy

pomegranates (POM•eh•gran•its): Fruit with red skin, sweet pulp, and seeds

scallop (SKAL•lup): A ribbed fan-shaped shell

trespass (TRESS•pass): Enter without permission

Wunderworld (WON•der•wurld): Home to Hades and Cerberus (Underworld in Greek mythology)

Questions

1. If you had magic winged sandals, where would you want to go?

2. Would you rather have winged sandals or a cap of invisibility? Why?

3. Aphrodite says that people tell her she's hard to like sometimes. Why do you think they say that? What are some things you like about her?

4. Do you think Persephone has bad luck-itis? Why or why not?

5. What new dangers do you think Athena, Persephone, and Aphrodite will come upon as they travel toward Sparkle City?

Authors' Note

Some of the ideas in the Little Goddess Girls books come from Greek mythology.

Persephone was the Greek goddess of plants and flowers. She divided her time between Earth and the Underworld, which she ruled with Hades. When she was in the Underworld it was winter on earth and not much could grow. Athena was the Greek goddess of wisdom. Aphrodite was the Greek goddess of love and beauty.

We also borrowed a few ideas from *The Wonderful Wizard of Oz*, a book written by L. Frank Baum. In that book, there is a road called the Yellow Brick Road. In this book, there is a Hello Brick Road. There are other similarities too. We've added lots of action and ideas of our own to this book too.

We hope you enjoy reading the Little Goddess Girls books!

—Joan Holub and Suzanne Williams